Bravo,
Max!

For Chris Haslam—
good on yer, mate!
—S. G.

Visit Sally Grindley's website: www.sallygrindley.co.uk

Aladdin Paperbacks
An imprint of Simon & Schuster Children's Publishing Division
1230 Avenue of the Americas, New York, New York 10020
This book is a work of fiction. Any references to historical events, real people, or real locales are used fictitiously. Other names, characters, places, and incidents are products of the author's imagination, and any resemblance to actual events or locales or persons, living or dead, is entirely coincidental.
Text copyright © 2005 by Sally Grindley
Illustrations copyright © 2005 by Tony Ross
First published in Great Britain by Orchard Books
First U.S. edition, 2007
Published by arrangement with Orchard Books,
a Division of Watts Publishing Group Ltd.
All rights reserved, including the right of reproduction in whole or in part in any form.
Aladdin Paperbacks and colophon are trademarks of Simon & Schuster, Inc.
The text for this book is set in Gill Sans and Goudy.
Manufactured in the United States of America
2 4 6 8 10 9 7 5 3 1
Library of Congress Cataloging-in-Publication Data
Grindley, Sally.
Bravo, Max! / by D.J. Lucas, aka Sally Grindley ;
[illustrations by Tony Ross.]—1st U.S. ed.
p. cm.
Summary: As he turns eleven years old, Max continues to exchange letters with his favorite author, from whom he receives some advice about writing a play and about coping with his mother's new boyfriend.
ISBN-13: 978-1-4169-0393-2 (hc)
ISBN-10: 1-4169-0393-3 (hc)
[1. Authorship—Fiction. 2. Friendship—Fiction. 3. Letters—Fiction.
4. Single-parent families—Fiction. 5. England—Fiction.] I. Ross, Tony, ill. II. Title.
PZ7.G88446Bra 2007
[Fic]—dc22
2005058378
ISBN-13: 978-1-4169-3645-9
ISBN-10: 1-4169-3645-9

Bravo, Max!

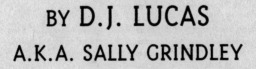

BY D.J. LUCAS

A.K.A. SALLY GRINDLEY

Aladdin Paperbacks · New York · London · Toronto · Sydney

To my friend Max

D.J.

Dear D.J.,

It's me again! Are you back from Australia yet?
I bet you missed my letters while you were
away. I had a great Christmas at Uncle Derek
and Pauline's. Their mad dog Scallywag stole
some of Gran's Christmas pudding when she
wasn't looking. Lucky it wasn't the bit with
the money in!

Thank you, thank you, thank you for your
postcard and for the signed copy of your new
book—*My Teacher's a Fruitcake*. I've already

read it and it's just as funny as *My Teacher's a Nutcase*. I love it when the teacher falls into the sandpit and a dog eats her shoes.

Have you made any New Year's resolutions? I made one. I was going to try not to step on any cracks in the pavement on my way to and from school, but I forgot and trod on one on the very first day! Doh!

Love, Max

P.S. You're still my favorite author.

Dear D.J.,

I don't think you can be home because you haven't written, but I'm going to keep writing until you write back—so there!

You'll never guess what. You know my Uncle Twinkle Toes Derek and his girlfriend Pauline, well, they belong to a theater club and they're in a play called *Cinderella and the Beanstalk* and Mum and I are going to see it. I bet it'll be amazing because Uncle Derek's in it.

Have you ever written a play? When I told my teacher, Miss Dimmer, that I was going to see a play, she said jolly good, because we'll be doing plays in class soon.

Hurry up and write, or I'll have to find a new favorite author!

Love, Max

P.S. We've got a soccer game on Saturday and I'm on the starting team. **YIPPEE!** Huge Bigbottom was rude about me being on the team, but he doesn't scare me. Just let him try!

January 21

Dear Max,

We're back. Phew! What a trip! Your two letters were waiting impatiently for me on the doormat, and I'm rushing to answer them because I don't want someone else taking over as your favorite author. Thank goodness you enjoyed My *Teacher's a Fruitcake*, or there might not have been any letters waiting!

We had a wonderful trip, Max. The highlight was walking over Sydney Harbour Bridge, which is so high it makes your stomach drop into your boots. I tried surfing for the first time, but I spent more time under the water making friends with the local fish than I did on my board. Christopher is a whiz at surfing, but he has flown to Australia lots of times so he's had plenty of practice. Now I must get down to some serious writing and thread all my research into my new story.

You sound really happy, Max. Well done for getting onto the soccer team. Just you prove Huge Bigbottom wrong.

Love, D.J.

P.S. I haven't written any plays, but one day . . . I just might.

Dear D.J.,

I'm **soooooo** glad you're back. It seemed like you were away forever!

Guess what, guess what, **GUESS WHAT!** Uncle Derek and Pauline have gotten engaged and they're going to get married this September! And guess what happened. In *Cinderella and the Beanstalk*, Uncle Derek played the giant and Pauline was Cinderella. The best bit was when Uncle Derek sat in the biggest custard pie you've ever seen just before he left for the ball. He was soooooo funny, Mum had tears rolling down her cheeks. She laughed just like she used to before Dad died.

Anyway, right at the end, when Cinderella danced with the prince, giant Uncle Derek pushed the prince out of the way and asked Cinderella—well, Pauline—to marry him. And she said yes. And everybody in the audience cheered like mad. Mum cried again because she was so happy and said if Dad had been there he would have called her a silly daft duck.

Love, Max

P.S. I nearly scored a goal in our soccer game, and I'm on the team again this week. Huge Bigbottom never passes to me, but Ben does because that's what best friends are for.

This is a picture of Uncle Derek with his big belly being a giant proposing to Pauline. Oh yes it is!

January 27

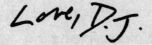

That's great news about Uncle Derek and Pauline. What a dramatic way to propose to someone. Thank goodness Pauline said yes!

Love, D.J.

Dear D.J.,

Seeing *Cinderella and the Beanstalk* has made me want to write a really, really, really funny play to make everyone laugh. And I like all the bits where the audience have to join in and shout things, especially when they have to boo the bad guy. Will you help me with it, please, please, please? I promise to help you with your new story too, like I did with *Dear Max* (hee hee!). When is *Dear Max* going to be published?

You haven't told me what's happening with your new story since you went to Australia to do research. Will it have kangaroos in it? **BOING! BOING! BOING!**

Love, Max

BOING

P.S. I've got a new friend at school. Her name's Emily, and she's got really, really, really long hair.

February 4

Dear Max,

Writing a play will be no problem for a boy with a big imagination like yours. You'll need a good plot and strong characters, but the plot will have to unfold through the words and actions of the characters on stage, rather than through description like in a story.

When you've thought about a subject for your play, decide how many characters you are going to have and write out a cast list, perhaps with a line about each person. But don't forget that you won't be able to fit too many people on stage at the same time. They might topple off or knock the scenery over!

I'm calling my new story *Where There's a Will*. It's about a boy named Will who is brilliant at surfing but has an accident that leaves him unable to walk. It's more serious than my other books, but it still has lots of funny moments, though no kangaroos so far.

Good luck with the play, Max.

Love, D.J.

P.S. I don't know when *Dear Max* is going to be published, but I've just heard that a very famous illustrator called Tony Ross is going to do the illustrations.

P.P.S. Say hello for me to Emily with the long hair.

Dear D.J.,

I can't wait to see Tony Ross's illustrations for
Dear Max. I looked at some of his books in the
library and he's the best.

Mum took me out to a restaurant last night. She's
got a new job working in a bank and she wanted
to celebrate, even though she said it doesn't
mean we're going to be millionaires.
We had such a brilliant time, D.J.
The food was delicious.
Our waiter called me
"Sir" and made me
feel like a grown-
up, so when we
stood up to go,

I said to Mum, "Would madam like to take my arm?" and she did. We walked all the way home like that, and when we went through the front door, Mum said, "Thank you, sir, you're a real gentleman." I love it when me and Mum act silly together.

Love, Max

P.S. I've decided to write a play about George and the dragon, except it's going to be called *Buster and the Dragon*.

P.P.S. How do I write my play out?

February 11

Dear Sir,

I understand Sir would like to know how to write out a play. He will be delighted to know that it is not a complicated exercise. He simply has to follow the example below:

MAX: I'm going to write a play
              about a boy who has to fight
              a dragon.

DRAGON: Will the dragon be fierce
              and scary but handsome?

MAX: The dragon will be the
              ugliest dragon ever seen.

DRAGON: Then the dragon will have
              to eat the boy before the
              boy can write his play!

(The dragon chases the boy, but the boy escapes. Smoke fills the stage as the dragon shows his anger.)

I do hope this will be of some help to Sir.

Kind regards, D.J.

P.S. You don't need to use speech marks, Max, and you need to put in parentheses all the notes about who is doing what on stage and any details about sound and lighting effects. Have fun!

February 12

Dear D.J.,

I can't believe your book *My Teacher's a Nutcase*
is being made into a film!!! It said so in the
newspaper this morning—Mum showed me.

Why didn't you tell me?
It's my favorite book of
all time and now there's
a film—YIPPEE! Does
that mean you're going
to be a movie star?!
You'll be an even more
famous author than
ever now. You will still
write to me, won't you?

Love, Max

February 15

Dear Max,

I am on my knees! I'm sorry I didn't tell you about the film. I just didn't want to talk about it until I knew for sure that it would go on general release.

I was asked if I would like to write the screenplay for My Teacher's a Nutcase—which is a bit like writing a play. It's much more complicated, though, and so different from writing a story that I threw my toys out of the pram and gave up. Someone else has written the script, and they've changed lots of things—including making the teacher a man instead of a woman!!! Tom Trews is going to be the teacher, and Jennifer Aniseed is going to be the school custodian!

I wouldn't dare stop writing to you, but I am disappearing under an avalanche of requests to do interviews and sign books, so don't tell me off if my letters are sometimes a bit brief.

Love, D.J.

Dear D.J.,

I can't believe they've changed your teacher into a man, especially Tom Trews! And I can't believe Jennifer Aniseed is going to be the grumpy old school custodian! Mum thinks it's really cheeky to change things like that, and so do I. They should keep what you wrote because it was your idea.

I've thought about the beginning of my play. Buster will be at home having breakfast with his mum when there's a great roar outside and lots of screams.

BUSTER: Perfect toast, Mum. Can I have some more, please?

MUM: What's that noise? I thought I heard a roar.

BUSTER: Someone's screaming.

(Looks out of the window.)

BUSTER: There's a dragon running down
                the street, Mum.
MUM: Quick, Buster, hide in the closet.
                I'm scared.

(While they're in the closet, the dragon
comes in, steals some toast from the
toaster, fills the room with smoke, then goes.
Buster comes out of the closet, is very cross
about losing his toast, and decides that the
dragon must be caught.)

Love, Max

February 21

Dear Max,

That's a great opening to your play. I can just see the dragon gallumping across the stage and stealing Buster's toast. Comedy and drama all in one go! Have you thought your plot right through to the end, and do you know about breaking it down into different scenes? Scenes are a bit like chapters and can be used to show a change of time or place, to move the action on or to change its pace.

What else is that dragon going to get up to and how is Buster going to deal with him? I'm intrigued.

Love, D.J.

P.S. You're right about Tom Trews playing the teacher in the film. He's not quite the mad middle-aged woman I had in mind!

Dear D.J.,

Uncle Derek has persuaded Mum to join his theater club, even though she says she can't act at all and would turn to jelly if she had to stand up in front of people. Uncle Derek says there are lots of other things she can do, like making costumes or painting scenery. Anyway, Uncle's taking her to a meeting tonight because he says it will do her good to get out, and Pauline is babysitting, even though I'm not a baby. WAAAAHHH!

It's just started to snow. YIPPEE! I hope it snows lots, then I can make a snowman.

Love, Max

P.S. The bad thing about snow is that we might not get to play our soccer game—it's the third time I've been picked!—and Mum was going to watch.

P.P.S. Have you met Tom Trews and Jennifer Aniseed yet?

Dear D.J.,

You should see the snow, D.J. It's like an alien world outside. I keep thinking a spaceship is about to land—**PLOOOF!** Pauline came to baby-sit with that silly mad dog Scallywag. He kept trying to catch the snow in his mouth. Jenny from my class, who lives in our apartment building, came to help us build a snow monster. She keeps wanting to be my best friend again, but she's not always nice to me, and anyway, I've got Ben and Emily.

Mum said she quite enjoyed herself with those theater people and asked if I would mind if she went again. I said of course I wouldn't, because I wouldn't, because I want her to be happy. She's a bit worried about going on her own, though, when Uncle Derek is away trucking. So I told her she had to be brave, like me.

Love, Max

P.S. In my play, Buster and his friends are going to be having a snowball fight on a soccer field, when the dragon arrives and melts all the snow with his fire.

February 28

Dear Max,

No snow so far. Lucky you. I adore snowball fights. My dotty cat Donut thinks snow is a type of bird and tries to catch it. Ambush just barks at it.

I love the idea of your dragon melting all the snow, but it might be difficult to make it happen on a stage without flooding the audience! Just something to bear in mind. . . . Some ideas are great in stories, and can be made to work in films using special effects, but are a problem in the theater.

I hope your soccer game wasn't canceled because of the snow or an invasion of snow monsters, and that you scored a million goals.

Love, D.J.

P.S. I haven't met Tom Trews and Jennifer Aniseed yet, but I'm going to watch some of the filming soon. I expect they'll be just as excited about meeting me!

Dear D.J.,

I can't believe you're really going to meet Tom
Trews and Jennifer Aniseed. You must be the
luckiest person in the whole world!

Mum's at her theater club tonight. I've got a new
babysitter because Pauline's at evening class and
Uncle Derek is trucking. She lives in our
apartment building and she's called Mrs. Burrows,
but I'm going to call her Mrs. Rabbits because
she talks a lot. She keeps asking me questions,
like what do I want to be when I grow up, and
all that sort of stuff that grown-ups always ask.
She's knitting and watching her favorite program
on TV at the moment and I've got to be quiet,
so I said I'd do some writing.

Our soccer game was canceled, but the snow has nearly all gone and it's cold and slushy and gray everywhere. Hope Mum comes home soon. Mrs. Rabbits has started talking again. This is a quick picture of her before she comes to look at what I'm doing.

Love, Max

March 6

Dear Max,

Does Mrs. Rabbits like carrots?! I used to have
a babysitter who never took her hat off! It was
a pale blue knitted woolen thing that she
pulled down to her ears. I always wondered
whether she had any hair underneath. Her
name was Mrs. Postlethwaite, and I used to
call her Bossy Possy because she was, and she
smelled of cabbage.

Have you thought about how many different
settings you are going to have in your play?
You can change them every time you have
a change of scene if you like, though it's better
not to make it too complicated. If the scene
changes take too long your audience will
fall asleep.

I must go. I feel inspired today, so I'm hoping to be able to hurtle forward with *Where There's a Will*.

Lots of love, D.J.

Dear D.J.,

It's Mum's theater night again. It's funny because
she didn't look like Mum when
she went out. She had new
clothes on and her hair
was sort of different.
I said to her, "Mum, you
look like a film star," and
she went bright red and
said, "That's very kind of
you, young man, but flattery
will get you nowhere." So
I said, "Will it get me as far
as a bowl of chocolate ice
cream?" and it did.

Mrs. Rabbits is here now. Mum asked me if I liked her and I said that she asks me loads of questions that I don't want to answer and that she says I'm small for my age, even though I've grown loads and I'm not the smallest in my class anymore. Mum said she's just trying to be friendly, but she should know that it's rude to talk about people's size, shouldn't she?

Jenny's just come round and Mrs. Rabbits says she can stay for an hour as long as we're quiet so she can watch her program on TV. Jenny asked if I would be her boyfriend. Yuck! I said I couldn't because she's taller than me. Anyway, I like Emily better (but that's a secret).

Love, Max

Dear D.J.,

Mum's out again. I wish the theater club didn't meet every week.

I tried to be friendly to Mrs. Rabbits. I asked her if Mr. Rabbits was at home, except that I forgot she was Mrs. Burrows and she gave me a funny look and asked me who "Mr. Rabbits" was. I didn't know what to say then, so I told her I needed to go to the bathroom. Now I'm in my room and I daren't go out. It's just as well I didn't ask her if she had any baby rabbits!

She's just been in and asked if I want to do a jigsaw puzzle with her. I said I was writing a letter and she looked at me all funny and said,

"Well, you're a weird one. I thought it was all e-mail these days." I told her we haven't got a computer and she went out—phew!

I think you might get a lot of long letters from me if I keep having to hide from Mrs. Rabbits!

She's come in again and said she doesn't like me being in my room on my own when she's there, even though I said that Mum doesn't mind. I suppose I'll have to go and do jigsaw puzzles with her, but all my puzzles are too babyish. Boring, boring, *boring*.

Love, Max

P.S. Mrs. Rabbits smells of straw.

March 18

Dear Max,

Keep your chin up, Max. At least you only have to put up with Mrs. Rabbits once a week and then she disappears back to her burrow.

I'm giving myself a great big pat on the back at the moment. I've finished the first three chapters of *Where There's a Will*. My writing's running away with me so fast that I can hardly keep up with it. I wish it was always like that. Will definitely has a few Max-like qualities—brave, determined—but not quite so handsome, of course. I'll have to make sure that Max doesn't creep surreptitiously into all of my books!

Love, D.J.

Dear D.J.,

I scored a goal on Saturday and Mum was watching! Huge Bigbottom was the only one who didn't say well done, but Ben was so pleased that he did a cartwheel across the field.

Mum bought me a new jigsaw puzzle. It's got a thousand pieces! That's the biggest jigsaw I've ever done, and the drawings of the animals are brilliant, especially the big old lion. I asked Mum

to help me because I like doing puzzles with
Mum. (I don't want to do it with Mrs. Rabbits!)

Mum asked if I minded if she went out for
a drink tomorrow night with some of her
friends from the theater club. I did mind a bit
because I didn't want Mrs. Rabbits to sit, but
I said I didn't mind, and Mum gave me a hug
and said Uncle Derek and Pauline had offered
to come—YIPPEE!

Love, Max

Dear D.J.,

Guess what, guess what, guess what! Uncle
Derek and Pauline want me to be a page boy at
their wedding! I'll get to dress up in a waistcoat
and bow tie and I'll be in nearly all the photos.
They said I'll be a V.I.P.—Very Important Person.

Mum's going to make my waistcoat for me.
We're going out with Pauline soon to choose
the material because she wants it to match
Uncle Derek's shirt.

I've done a bit more of my play. This is the
beginning of scene number two, after the
dragon has been back again and all the people
in the village are terrified.

SCENE TWO

(In Buster's garden. Buster is sharpening a piece of wood and cleaning his Frisbee.)

BUSTER'S MUM: Please, Buster, don't go. Stay and look after your poor mother. Your father's already been eaten by one dragon. Let someone else fight that horrible dragon.

BUSTER: It's no good, mother. I am the only boy brave enough to fight that dragon, so fight it I must, or nobody will ever be able to eat toast safely again.

BUSTER'S MUM: Can't we just run away?

BUSTER: No, Mum. Running away is what
              cowards do.

Love, Max

P.S. You see, I remembered your book *Who's
Afraid of the Big Bad Boy?* and what the girl
said to the bully. You can't run away just
because you're frightened.

March 27

Dear V.I.P.

I love the bit of your play you sent me. You've already set up the direction in which the story is going and introduced your main characters, which is important. You've had lots of action with the dragon frightening the villagers; now perhaps you could move to a new setting to see what the dragon will do next.

I was in a school play once. I played Briar Rosebud and I had to throw my arms round Prince Charming. My bracelet caught on his collar and I couldn't pull myself away. We were stuck together! I got the giggles then and ruined what should have been a very romantic moment—especially since I had a big crush on the boy who was playing Prince Charming.

Love, D.J.

P.S. Congratulations on the goal, Max. David Beckham had better watch out!

Dear D.J.,

Mum's gone to the theater club and Mrs. Rabbits is here. She's taken over my puzzle and she's doing the big old lion. I wanted to do him, but she said it was too difficult for me. Then she said the easiest bit was the tree and that I should do that. I told her I'd rather do some writing, so she gave me that funny look again and shook her head. I couldn't help myself when she did that. I said, "I'm writing to my friend who's a very famous author," and she said, "Are you, dear? That's nice." I could tell she didn't believe me, though, and that she still thinks I'm weird.

I thought she was going to do my puzzle all evening and there'd be nothing left for me

and Mum, but she's watching her favorite
program now, so I've got to be quiet.
I feel like making as much noise as I can just to
annoy her, because she annoys me all the time.

Love, Max

P.S. It's the morning now. I've undone all the
bits of jigsaw that Mrs. Rabbits
did, so now I can do the
big old lion myself.
So there.

April 3

Dear Max,

That big old rabbit is certainly a pain in the burrow. You'll have to throw yourself into your playwriting when she's there and try to ignore her. If only you could tell her to hop it!

I'm about to go to Milan to watch some of the filming of My *Teacher's a Nutcase*. It's all very exciting, and rather scary. Christopher says I'll be fine, but I'm sure I shall say something completely idiotic when I'm introduced to the stars.

Love, D.J.

April 4

Dear D.J.,

Mum's got a new friend. His name's James, and he knows Uncle Derek because he is in the theater club as well. He took Mum out for a drink last night, but I didn't see him. Uncle Derek babysat. Lucky it wasn't Mrs. Rabbits, because with Uncle Derek I could watch soccer on TV.

Uncle Derek says James is a very nice man, and I asked if he was Mum's boyfriend. Uncle said that at the moment he is just someone who makes Mum laugh. I told him that I make Mum laugh too.

Uncle Derek makes all of us laugh. Pauline says he's like one of those balls with a squeaker inside, only ten times the size and one hundred times as bouncy. When he was babysitting, he

took a Ping-Pong ball from his pocket and said
he wanted to play table tennis. He stood some
books across the middle of the kitchen table for
the net and we had a
dustpan and a saucepan
lid as paddles.

You should have seen us, D.J.
I couldn't reach anything in the
middle of the table because I'm too short, and
Uncle Derek couldn't reach because of his big
fat belly. Uncle Derek smashed one ball so
hard that it landed in the butter dish—**SPLAT!**
And then he crunched against the table and
broke one of the legs off! We both got the

giggles and lay on the floor for ages, then we had to spend the rest of the evening putting the table back together.

Love, Max

P.S. I'm going to have a big fat knight in my play who's going to protect Buster's mum while he's away and stop her from being sad.

P.P.S. The table wobbles now.

Caro Max
Greetings from MILAN, where the sun is
shining and the rich and famous have
been rubbing shoulders with me. I've
just watched the filming of the scene
where the wasp is caught in the
teacher's hair. Tom Trews is
wearing an enormous curly wig and
it's hilarious. I'm being treated rather
like royalty. Everyone wants to take
me out to dinner, and I've eaten so
much pasta that Christopher has
starting calling me D.J. Lucasetti.
I hope you like the picture on the
front of the card. It's by a very
famous artist called Michelangelo,
who is even better than Tony Ross.
          Love D.J.

Max
30 Sharpener Street
Anytown
MX9 3BT

Hello Max
Jennifer Aniseed

Hello Max
Tom Trews

Dear D.J.,

Thank you, thank you, **THANK YOU** for my postcard and for Tom Trews's and Jennifer Aniseed's autographs. Everyone at school will be soooooo jealous when I show them.

I'm on my spring break, and I've been with Mum and Pauline to choose the material for my waistcoat and bow tie and to buy Uncle Derek's shirt. Uncle Derek wants Pauline to surprise him with it. I said it would be a big surprise if we bought him a bright red shirt! We didn't, though. We bought light blue shirts, and the material for my waistcoat and bow tie is dark blue and shiny.

Mum and I had lunch at Uncle Derek's and guess who was there . . . James, you know,

Mum's friend that I told you about. He's got a
beard! He wears a jacket with patches on the
elbows and he drives a silly old sports car. He's
an architect, but I don't think he can have
much money if he's got patches.

He's not as good at soccer as Uncle Twinkle
Toes Derek, even though Uncle's got a big fat
belly. He gave Mum a kiss on the cheek when
we left. **Yuck!** Fancy being kissed by a man
with a beard! I'm going to call him Hairychops.

When I said to Mum that he must be poor because of his patches and his silly old sports car, she said that he wasn't poor but that clothes and cars weren't important to him. He must be crazy. If I had plenty of money, I wouldn't have patches, and I would buy a brand-new **soooooper dooooper** sports car. I bet your Christopher has a soooooper dooooper sports car, being as he flies jumbo jets.

Love, Max

P.S. This is me with a big fat belly after eating four Easter eggs.

P.P.S. Scallywag stole one of my Easter eggs and was very, very sick. Ugh!

April 17

Dear Max,

You're right. Christopher does have a sooooper
dooooper sports car, and it terrifies me! When
he puts his foot on the accelerator, it leaves my
stomach behind! I certainly wouldn't like to be
kissed by someone with a beard. They're all
tickly and full of bits of boiled egg!

If you're going to have scenes in your play with
Buster's mum and her fat knight friend, how
are you going to get them off the stage before
Buster starts chasing the dragon? Remember
that if you have a big scene change, you might
have to have lots of people running backward
and forward with props, as well as different
backdrops and lighting.

I'm doing a radio interview about the film in a few minutes' time, so I must fly.

Love, D.J.

Dear D.J.,

Mum's gone to the movies with James.
I wanted to go too, but Mum said the film is
too old for me. Mrs. Rabbits is here for the
second day in a row. She started to ask me
about my dad and did I still miss him and she
expected that I would like a new dad and that
Mum must be lonely all on her own. I said
that Mum wasn't all on her own because she's
got me!

Love, Max

P.S. In my play there's going to be a gruesome
ogre that lives under the ground and keeps
popping up to stop Buster from getting to
the dragon.

OGRE: Who's that stomp stomping across my land?

BUSTER: It's me, Buster. I'm going to catch a dragon.

OGRE: Not across my land you're not. All that stomp stomp stomping when I'm trying to watch TV. Go and catch a dragon somewhere else and stop being a pest.

BUSTER: I wasn't stomp stomping and I'm not a pest.

OGRE: All boys are pests.

April 24

Dear Max,

It sounds as if Mrs. Rabbits has rather large feet
and likes to put them in things. Keep that
imagination working, Max, and you'll be able
to magic her out of your house and off into
a field miles away from you! I like the ogre.
Who else is going to pop up in your plot?

Love, D.J.

Dear D.J.,

Mum asked if I mind if James has lunch with us on Sunday. I said I don't, but I do, because I like having Mum to myself for Sunday lunch, unless Uncle Derek and Pauline come round. I hope he doesn't stay long, because there's a wildlife program about tigers on TV, and Mum and I always watch the wildlife programs together like we used to with Dad. I expect Hairychops won't want to watch it, so Mum won't let me, either, because it would be rude.

Love, Max

P.S. Emily's my other best friend now, so I told
her about Mrs. Rabbits and she gave me a bar
of chocolate.

P.P.S. In my play, I'm going to have a bearded
knight called Fungus Face who wants to catch
the dragon and steal all the glory from Buster.

Dear D.J.,

We went to a wildlife park after lunch on
Sunday. Hairychops took us in his silly old
sports car and I sat in this tiny seat
in the back. I was all crunched
up. Mum's hat blew away and
she thought it was really
funny and said at least
it wasn't a wig.
I thought she'd
be upset.

Hairychops doesn't know much about animals,
not like my dad did, so I had to keep telling
him what the animals were. Can you believe
he'd never even heard of a meerkat?! He
bought me a furry raccoon. (He thought it was

a badger!) It's really babyish.
He bought Mum a tiny
bear key ring and she's
put all her keys onto it.
I think it's stupid.

When Hairychops went
home, he shook hands with
me and said, "I've learned a lot, thank you,
Max." Then he gave Mum another kiss on the
cheek. Yuck!

Love, Max

P.S. Mum recorded the tiger program, so we
didn't miss it. **GRRRR!**

P.P.S. I did what you said and imagined Mrs.
Rabbits far away in a field when she came last
night. She got chased by a fox and fell down
a well. Ha!

May 10

Dear Max,

Poor Mrs. Rabbits. Fancy being chased by a fox.

I'm amazed that Hairychops hadn't heard of a meerkat. Even I've heard of a meerkat, and I'm not exactly an expert on wildlife. I soon will be, though. Christopher and I have decided to go on safari to South Africa this December, after I've finished *Where There's a Will* and all the fuss about *My Teacher's a Nutcase* has died down. So watch out, Max, I'll be testing you when I come back!

I've just heard that the film of *My Teacher's a Nutcase* is going to be released here on December 7. They're doing all the special effects at the moment.

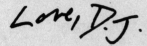

P.S. Do you think Hairychops is hiding something under his beard—like a big mole?!

Dear D.J.,

I think Hairychops is hiding a big family of moles under his beard!

I can't believe you're going on safari! I'd never eat a burger again if it meant I could go on safari! You'll see lions and elephants and crocodiles and hippopottymouses and giraffes and laughing hyenas (yuck!). No tigers, though—you can't catch me out there.

I can't wait to see your film. Will we be able to see it where we live? There is a movie theater nearby, but it's a bit old and tumblydown and sometimes the film starts to wobble and the music goes all crackly. Or we could go to the big theater in the middle of town and have popcorn and ice cream, but it's a bit expensive.

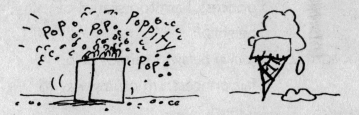

I asked Mum if Emily could come and see the film with us as well as Ben and Uncle Derek and Pauline, and she said yes. So that means you've got six people coming already, which is a good start.

Love, Max

P.S. I'm going to have a princess for Buster to save in my play.

PRINCESS: Help! Help! O woe is me! I am stuck in my castle and I need to get out to rescue my cat, which is stuck up in yonder tree. Please get me down before the dragon returns.

KNIGHT 1: (*down below*) I cannot help, fair princess. I am too scared of heights.

KNIGHT 2: (*down below*) I cannot help, fair princess. I'm on my way to a joust.

FUNGUS FACE: (*down below*) I would help, fair princess, but my beard will catch in the tree.

Dear Max,

You're really getting into the spirit of your play! I love the knights and especially the idea of Fungus Face getting caught in a tree by his beard. What a motley crew! I'm being taken out tonight by the director and producer of "My Teacher's a Nutcase" to help promote the film. On "My Teacher's a Nutcase" they've gone in to help promote the film. On with the high heels and lipstick again.

Love, D.J.

P.s. I'm sure "My Teacher's a Nutcase" will be at your movie theater. I'll find out nearer the time and let you know.

Dear D.J.,

Mum's got a big birthday on June 29. She's going to be forty and doesn't want to be reminded. Uncle Derek's planning a party for her, and Gran and Grandad are coming.

What do you think I should buy her, D.J.? I've saved up a bit of money, but it's not very much. Gran said what about some chocolates, but Mum's on a diet, and Pauline said what about a purse, because Mum's old one is tatty. But I want to get her something that tells her I love her and that she's the best. I can't afford a ring, except a plastic one, so what else?

Love, Max

May 31

Dear Max,

Lucky Mum—only forty. Have you thought
about buying your mum some flowers, Max?
Flowers are a lovely way to tell somebody how
much you love them and would make your
mum feel very special.

Love, D.J.

Dear D.J.,

Flowers are a brilliant
idea, and Pauline agrees.
She said she'd help me
buy them, and at the
same time I can
help her choose
her flowers for the
wedding. It made
me feel really
grown-up and
important.

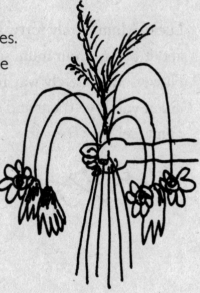

Mrs. Rabbits sat last night and I imagined her
with long, floppy ears and a fluffy white tail and
a twitchy nose every time she rabbited at me.

I twitched my nose back at her once and she gave me her *You are really a weird boy* look, then I got the giggles and she said, "If you're going to be silly, you can go to your room." So I went. Mum was at the theater club, but at least Hairychops is away for a week, so I've got Mum to myself—YIPPEE!

Love, Max

That's the spirit, Max.
A quick twitch of the
nose works wonders.
I must try it myself.

Love, D.J.

Dear D.J.,

Mum and me went to this **HUGE** park with Uncle Derek and Pauline and Ben. It had a miniature train running right the way round it pulled by a real steam engine. I didn't think the engine would be strong enough to pull Uncle Derek, but it did! There were lots of rides to go on as well. We went on the log flumes, and me and Ben leaned out so that we got soaked. Then I gave Mum a hug so that she was all wet as well. Ben thinks my family is cool.

Love, Max

P.S. Hairy chops is back the day after tomorrow - Boooo! We have much more fun without him.

D.J. Lucas
30 Pencil Drive
Writingdom
DJ1 0AU

Dear D.J.,

I've been thinking about my play. The fat knight falls asleep and Buster's mum sets off to find Buster. Fungus Face sees her and decides to take her prisoner.

BUSTER: Go home, Mum, and shut all the doors and don't let anyone in except me and the fat knight.

BUSTER'S MUM: I'm scared for us, Buster. What if the dragon carries you away and I never see you again?

BUSTER: Never fear, Mother. That dragon won't get the better of me. I shall fight him with my trusty sword,

and if that doesn't work, I shall use
my Frisbee. It is Fungus Face I am
afraid of. Don't let him near you.

(In a shady place nearby.)

FUNGUS FACE: I'll soon put a stop to that
interfering boy's plans to get rid of
me. I'm going to capture his mum
and take her miles away across the
fields so that he can't find her.

OGRE: You can take her across *my* fields if
you wish, Mr. Fungus Face. That
boy is a pest and needs to be
taught a lesson.

(They shake hands and do wicked laughter so
that the audience boos.)

Love, Max

P.S. Mrs. Rabbit Poo is sitting tonight because
Mum's going out for a meal with Hairychops.

June 18

Dear Max,

So your two bad guys are going to join forces.
What a scary thought! You'll have your
audience cowering under their seats. I hope
Buster's mum will be all right. Is your big fat
knight going to save her, or is Buster going to
save his mum from Fungus Face and kill the
dragon as well? He's got a busy time ahead
of him.

I'm about to nip off to Paris now for two days.
My French publisher wants me to do a round
of book signings. Paris is my favorite city, so
I'm looking forward to it. . . .

Love, D.J.

Dear D.J.,

Hairychops was here yesterday. Mum asked him round for lunch, worse luck. I asked him how old he was, and he's four years younger than Mum. (Mum said it was a bit rude, but I thought it was only rude to ask a lady.) He doesn't look younger with that beard. He looks YEARS older. He's a bit serious and he asks me serious questions, but he thinks he's funny. He's nowhere near as funny as Uncle Derek or my dad.

When he'd gone, I asked Mum if Hairychops (I didn't call him that!) was her boyfriend, and she said that she supposed he sort of was. I didn't know what to say then, because I don't want him to keep coming round, because I like having Mum to myself. And if she loves Hairychops she might not love me as much anymore. She gave me a big hug, though, and told me I would always be her number one man, but I don't want there to be another man as well, especially when it means I keep having to have Mrs. Rabbits.

Love, Max

Cher Max,

Greetings from Paris, where the sun is shining and the streets are paved with tables and chairs and the smell of strong coffee. I just love sitting at a pavement café and watching the world go by. My hand is stiff from signing hundreds of books — I seem to be quite popular over here.

A bientôt

D. J.

Max
30 Sharpener Street
Anytown
MX9 3BT

PARIS

Dear D.J.,

I hate Hairychops. Hate him, hate him, HATE HIM. I gave Mum my flowers, and she gave me a big kiss and said they were beautiful and that she loved me very much. Then Hairychops had to go and spoil it. We went to Uncle Derek's for the party, and Hairychops turned up with a HUGE bunch of red roses. I didn't even know he was going to be there, and—you'll never believe it—he had shaved his beard off! It made my flowers look silly, and Mum won't mind if he kisses her now he's a **BALDYCHOPS**. And if he gave her a huge bunch of roses, that means he's trying to pretend that he loves her more than I do, so he's a liar because he can't, because I've known her forever and he's only just met her.

Now everyone's all upset with me—even
Gran and Grandad—because I hid in the
closet under the stairs so that no one could
find me, until Uncle Derek found
me, but I didn't want to speak to him or
anyone else.

Mum won't love me now and it's all
Baldychops's fault. I hate him, hate him,
hate him!

Love, Max

Dear Max,   July 3

You didn't tell me if there was a big family of moles under Baldychops's beard. I bet there was at least one, poor thing.

Max, I hope you will be feeling better by the time you read this. Have you talked to Pauline about why you were upset? I'm sure she would understand, because she helped you to buy the flowers.

One thing I do know is that your mother will always love you more than anyone else, no matter how many roses they give her.

So chin up, Max, and keep a lookout for those moles!

Love, D.J.

July 9

Dear D.J.,

Mum had a big chat with me and said I had
upset her very much on her birthday. She
wanted to know what was wrong, but I didn't
know what to say. I just said that someone had
been horrible to me at school and I was in
a bad mood. She wanted to know who, so
I said it was Jenny but that she wasn't to say
anything because it would make things worse.
Now I feel awful because I told a big whopper
to my mum. Jenny deserves it, though, because
she's started saying things at school about
Mum having a boyfriend.

I wish Baldychops would just go away and
then things could go back to the way
they were.

At least it's nearly summer vacation. I'm going to Cornwall with Gran and Grandad and Ben's coming with me. At least I won't have to see Baldychops or Mrs. Rabbit Poo, but I'll miss Emily.

Love, Max

P.S. There was a mole hiding. It's quite small but I imagine it growing and growing until it takes over his whole face and turns it into a big brown blob.

P.P.S. In my play, Fungus Face captures Buster's mum, and with the help of a wicked witch he casts a spell on her to make her think he's the most wonderful knight in all the land.

July 14

Dear Max,

We all tell whoppers sometimes, Max, to
protect people we love. Yours was quite
a little whopper compared to one or two
enormous great whoppers I've told because
I haven't wanted to hurt someone. As long
as it doesn't become a habit. We don't want
your nose growing.

Forget about everything while you're away in
Cornwall, apart from sending me a postcard.
You will not be forgiven if you forget that!

Be brave, Max.

Love, D.J.

P.S. There's a seal sanctuary in Cornwall, which you would love. I certainly won't be seeing any seals on my safari.

Dear D.J.,

Baldychops came round for lunch again.
I decided to be nice to him because I didn't
want to upset Mum. He asked if he could read
my play. I didn't really want him to, because
I thought he would think it was silly. Mum
persuaded me, and do you know what? He said
he would help me with it if I wanted him to.
I said no, thank you very much, because you're
helping me, and he said in that case I was very
lucky and didn't need him. He did a drawing of
my dragon and he's better at drawing than
sport. Mum showed him some of my drawings,
even though I told her not to, and he said they
were really good, but I bet he didn't mean it.

Love, Max

Dear D.J.,

We finished school today. YIPPEE! It's not long till I go on vacation, and then it won't be long till Uncle Derek and Pauline's wedding, and then it'll be my birthday—and yours. I'm thinking about all the things I've got to look forward to.

Love, Max

P.S. In my play, Buster comes home to see if his mother is all right before going after the dragon again. Fungus Face pretends to be all nice and cuddly, but Buster knows he's faking it because he wants to take his mother prisoner.

FUNGUS FACE: Hello, Buster. How nice to see you. Would you like a toasted crumpet?

BUSTER: I'd like two, please, with butter and honey.

FUNGUS FACE: (to the ogre) Look after our friend, will you?

(Fungus Face goes offstage. Ogre tries to grab Buster.)

BUSTER: Leave me alone, you ugly brute.

(He pushes the ogre into a closet.)

That's taken care of her.

(Goes to Fat Knight, who is snoring in the corner.)

Wake up, Fat Knight. We've got to
get rid of Fungus Face so that
Mum will be safe and I can go and
fight the dragon.

(The Fat Knight carries on snoring.)

Doh! Then I'll have to do it on
my own.

July 25

Dear Max,

He's a feisty little character, your Buster, isn't he? I wouldn't like to tangle with him! Have you thought about asking your friends to act out your play when you've finished it? A play only comes to life when actors jump into the roles and interpret the characters in their own way. I'm sure your teacher would be thrilled if you and your friends were to act it out in front of the rest of the class. That's something for you to think about over summer vacation— who should play what part.

I'm flying to New York tomorrow for five days. I'm going to be signing books in bookshops and libraries. It's all part of the publicity for

My Teacher's a Nutty Fruitcake. Between you and me, I'd much rather stay at home and relax in my garden than shoot off to the other side of the world to stay in a boring hotel. Look out for the New York postcard, though I'll be back before it reaches you!

Love, D.J.

Dear D.J.,

I know you're not there, but I wanted to tell
you that I think your idea about my play is
brilliant. I think I'm going to let Ben be Buster.
Mum said we could even dress up and she
would help with some costumes. Baldychops
said he'd help with props, but I said no thank
you, because my friends would want to do
them. Anyway, they'd be Baldyprops! (Get it?)

Mrs. Rabbits sat last night. She wouldn't let me
watch soccer again, so when she went to
make a cup of tea, I pulled her knitting off the
needles (ha!). She sent me to bed early, but
I didn't care, because I didn't want to be in the
same room as her. As long as she doesn't
tell Mum.

I just can't wait to go on vacation now, far
away from annoying rabbits and James the
Pain. I wish I was going to New York like you.
That would be far away enough. I can't wait to
add your New York postcard to my collection.

Love, Max

Dear D.J.,

I'm off on vacation tomorrow—YIPPEE! Ben's staying the night so that we can leave very early, and Uncle Derek is driving us all the way down the motorway to meet up with the wrinklies. (Hee hee, that's what Uncle Derek calls them when no one else is listening!) Uncle Derek says it'll take us hours to get to Cornwall the way Grandad drives, so the earlier we set off the better.

I can't wait for Ben to get here.

I asked Mum if she would be all right on her own, because she can't come because she's too busy at work. She said she would find it very, very hard and would pine like mad, but she would survive the heartache as long as she knew I was having a wonderful time. And then she said that, seriously, she would miss me but she was sure that James would help her through it. I didn't like that, and it made me not want to go because I don't want Baldychops to try and take my place, but Mum said it wouldn't be the same without me, so I felt a bit better.

Love, Max

I was here →

Dear Max
Having a hectic time. I'm being
shuttled so quickly from book
signing to drinks reception to
party that my feet have
hardly touched the ground.
Christophe's flying in tonight, so
I've demanded a night off so we
can go and have a quiet meal
together, but he's flying straight
back to England next day. New
York is amazing. My neck is
stiff from looking up at all
the sky scrapers.'

Love, D.J.

NEW YORK
PM 2007

Max
30 Sharpener Street
Anytown
MX1 3BT

Dear DJ. My turn to send a postcard.
King Arthur lived in the castle on
the front of this card! Not much
of it left, is there! I might have
a king in my play. He could pay
the dragon a lot of money for
getting rid of Fungus Face because
he doesn't want him in his kingdom.
We went to see that seal sanctuary
you said. It was brilliant
seeing the seals so close. The hotel's
got a big swimming pool, so I have
races with Ben and he always
wins because he's faster than me.
Gran and Grandad lie by the
pool and snore.
          Love, Max

D.J. Lucas
30 Pencil Drive
Writingdom
DJ1 · OAU

I was
here

ARTHUR'S CASTLE   TINTAGEL

Dear D.J.,

I'm back. Did you miss me?! Mum did. When she opened the door I gave her the biggest hug in the whole wide world, and she gave me the biggest hug in the whole wide world back. Baldychops wasn't there, thank goodness.

We had a brilliant vacation. We went to the beach and we went fishing and Ben and me tried surfing but we kept falling off. Grandad said he took my dad to lots of the places we

went to. He said Dad was a goof because
he liked to hide, then jump out and shout,
"**BOO!**" Gran said it didn't matter how many
times he did it, it always made her jump.
I laughed thinking about Dad doing that,
so I did it myself and Gran nearly jumped out
of her skin. I told them about my play, because
I thought my dragon might jump out and say,
"**BOO!**" I said about Mum and the theater
club, but I didn't say anything about Baldychops
because I didn't want to think about him
trying to take my place.

Everyone's excited about the wedding now.
Only three weeks to go.

Love, Max

P.S. Are you going to marry your Christopher?
Mum says that's an incredibly cheeky thing to
ask, but you don't have to answer if you don't
want to.

August 20

Dear Max,

Thank you for your postcard, Max. It sounds
as if you had a wonderful vacation. Your poor
gran, having to cope with one scallywag
after another!

Christopher and I don't have any plans to
get married, but I didn't mind your asking.
We both like being free to scuttle back to
our own shells. When I'm in the middle of
writing a book, I'm probably best left alone
anyway. I can be very grumpy if it's not going
well. Even Donut and Ambush cower in
a corner then.

Love, D.J.

Dear D.J.,

Mum's finished my waistcoat and bow tie.
I look like a really cool dude in them. This is
a picture of me.

Da Daaa

This is the shortest letter I've ever written
to you!

Love, Max

August 30

Dear Dude,

I bet you'll be the coolest dude at the wedding.
Give my very best wishes to Uncle Derek and
Pauline. I hope you all have a fantastic day,
and I look forward to seeing a photograph of
the cool dude.

Love, D.J.

Dear D.J.,

Uncle Derek and Pauline's wedding was
brilliant. Pauline looked like a movie star. It
was the first time I'd seen Uncle in a suit.
It covered his big fat belly up quite well. I felt
very important being with them at the front
of the church. Baldychops had to sit behind
us with all the Not-So-Important-People
(N.S.I.P.s). Ha!

I didn't like the photo bit. It went on and on
and on. I was at the top table afterward at the
hotel and Mum let me try some champagne. It
was YUCK! The bubbles went straight up my
nose and made me sneeze.

Baldychops kept putting his arm round Mum, and when they danced together they were all lovey-dovey. I don't want him thinking he can marry my mum just because Uncle and Pauline got married. I made Mum dance with me and we did disco dancing with bumping bottoms, not smoochy stuff.

School starts in four days' time. I don't want to go back. We'll have a new teacher, but I want to stay with Miss Dimmer. The new teacher might not let me do my play. I hope I'll be on the soccer team again.

Love, Max

P.S. I'll send you a photo of the cool dude.

September 5

Dear Max,

It sounds as if the wedding went really well.
You're right about the photo bit. I hate having
my photo taken. Unfortunately, at the moment
everyone wants photos of me. Ah, the price
of fame!

Talking of fame, I've just been invited to
Hollywood to see a preview of My *Teacher's
a Nutcase*. There's a place there called the
Walk of Fame, where the names of famous stars
are etched into star-shaped plaques embedded
in the paving stones. Christopher says he'll
steal out at midnight and etch my name.

I hope your new teacher is even better than Miss Dimmer and encourages you to finish your play and perform it.

Love, D.J.

Dear D.J.,

I can't believe you're going to Hollywood! You must be **AMAZINGLY** famous. Please, please, please will you send me a Hollywood postcard?

I told my friends your idea about doing my play at school. They got really excited and they want to make the props as well, so we don't need Baldychops. Ben can't wait to be Buster, and Emily went all pink when I asked her to be the princess. I told Jenny she could be a wicked witch, but she stuck her tongue out at me. I'm going to be the dragon so I can breathe fire over everyone!

I'm on the soccer team again this term and we've got our first match next week. I'm going to score a million goals, and Mum will be watching and she'll cheer like mad because she'll be so proud of me.

Mum's out at the theater tonight and the Rabbit's coming. I'm going to ignore her and do the final cast list for my play and decide who's playing which part, and I'm going to write a list of the props we need so far.

Love, Max

P.S. Our new teacher is called Mr. Hatch, but I call him Eggy in my head because he's quite grumpy. He'd better not stop us from doing my play.

September 14

Dear Dragon,

Watch you don't set fire to your letters!

I'm so pleased all your friends want to be
involved in your play. It'll certainly keep you
busy if you're going to do all the props and
scenery yourselves.

I am really, really busy. I'm being called all the
time by newspapers wanting to do interviews
with me about the film. A new edition of
My *Teacher's a Nutcase* is about to come
out, with a cover showing the stars in the
film—including Tom Trews as the teacher
(yes, the inside of the book has had to be
changed as well).

I must finish *Where There's a Will* before we go away in December, so back to work. . . .

Have a great birthday, Max. It's worked out that I shall be in Hollywood for my birthday. It all seems incredibly unreal.

Love, D.J.

Have a wonderful day, Max.
Eleven years old!
Do NoT open parcel until
the 18th.

Birthday
Wishes

Dear D.J.,

Thank you sooooooo much
for my present. I've been
taking pictures of everybody!
SNAP SNAP SNAP! Mum and
Uncle Derek and Pauline bought me
a computer—**WHOOPEEEE!**—and Uncle
Derek's going to show me how to put my
photographs on it. Mum said that you had written
to check if I would like a camera, so thank you
again, D.J. I'm not going to start e-mailing you,
though. I like writing letters, and I like getting
them even more.

Baldychops gave me a set of paints and
brushes and some paper for doing paintings.
Mum says it's the best paper you can get
for painting.

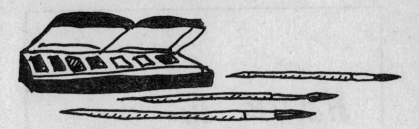

Baldychops and Mum took me bowling with
Ben, then we went for a birthday meal. I wish
it had been with Uncle Derek and Pauline
instead of Baldychops, but they've only just got
back from their honeymoon. I'm terrible at
bowling, and you'll never believe it but
Baldychops was the best, even though he's
awful at sports. At least he didn't try to hold
Mum's hand or anything, because I didn't want
Ben to see them.

Love, Max (Age 11)

P.S. I hope you liked the special card I did for
you and that you had a fantastico birthday
in Hollywood.

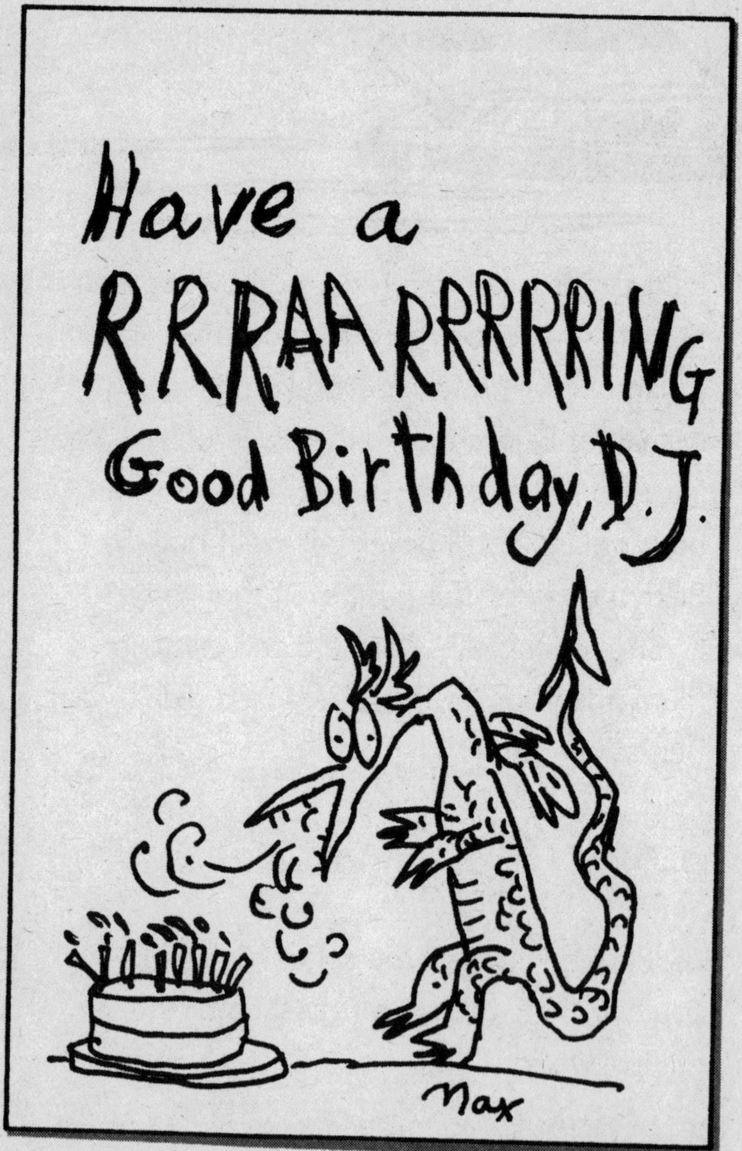
Have a
RRRAARRRRRING
Good Birthday, D.J.
Max

Greetings from Hollywood, Max.
I can't believe I've just written
that! We walked along the Walk
of Fame. There are so many
famous names from yesterday and
today, including Tom Trews.
The film is brilliant, even though
they've changed lots of things,
and everybody thinks it will
be a big hit.
I hope you had a fantastic
birthday, and I look forward
to reading all about it when
I'm home.
        Love, D.J.

Max
30 Sharpener Street
Anytown
   MX9 3BT

Dear D.J.,

I hate Jenny Wheeler. She's told everybody
that Mum's got a boy toy and that she saw
them kissing and holding hands like they were
a couple of kids. I said that Baldychops is only
Mum's friend and that they do theater
together, but Jenny said they do more than
that together and made everyone laugh.
Now it's all horrible again at school. Ben said
I should ignore Jenny because she's always
making trouble, but I didn't want people like
Huge Bigbottom knowing things about my
mum, and I didn't want Emily to think my
mum's a bad person.

Love, Max

Dear D.J.,

I wish Mrs. Rabbits would
hop it. She's all yucky
sickly sweet when Mum's
around, but as soon as
Mum goes she turns into
a monster. She got really
cross with me last night
because I wanted to watch
soccer on TV and she said I
couldn't because she wanted to
watch her soap and I said it was my house so I
should be able to choose. She yelled at me for
being cheeky and said she would tell Mum.

I hate Mrs. Rabbits. And I hate Jenny. And I
hate Baldychops because it's all his fault.

Love, Max

October 1

Dear Max,

Jenny's obviously cross because you asked her
to be a wicked witch in your play and not
a princess, so she's trying to hurt you back.
Don't let her, Max. Ben's right. Ignore her.
As for Mrs. Rabbits, I suppose she might
believe she had as much right to watch what
she wanted, though I'm hoping the silly old
bat might have felt too ashamed about
making a fuss over a television program
to tell your mother.

Be strong, Max.

Love, D.J.

Dear D.J.,

We've got a game tomorrow and Mum said
she'd watch, but she asked if Baldychops could
come too because he'd like to. I don't want
him to, D.J., because it'll be embarrassing and
they might hold hands. I said to Mum that I like
it when she comes on her own or with Uncle
Derek, and she said, "But you like James, don't
you?" So I had to say he was all
right. I didn't want to say
anything else then in
case I upset Mum, but
I think I upset her
anyway, because she
said she'd come on her
own but she didn't look
very happy. So I said
I didn't mind if he came,

but I do mind. I'm not looking forward to the
game now, and I hope I'm not well so that
I can't play.

Love, Max

Dear D.J.,

It's all so **HORRIBLE**. Mum came to watch the match with Baldychops, and Jenny went and stood with them and talked to them. I couldn't concentrate on playing football because I kept wondering what they were saying. Even Ben got cross with me because I kept miskicking the ball. Huge Bigbottom said I was useless and it was my fault that we let in a goal. Then he said, "Is that your mum's boy toy?" I kicked him, D.J., and I wanted to kick him again and again, but Ben pulled me away. My teacher saw it and sent me off. Mum looked really upset. At the end of the match, Mum and Baldychops started to walk over to me, so I pretended not to see them and ran into the school and hid.

We lost the match because of me. My teacher
yelled at me, and he's dropped me from the
team.

I just want things to be like they were, D.J., just
me and Mum.

Love, Max

October 17

Dear Max,

Jenny really has got it in for you, hasn't she,
and Huge Bigbottom still seems to be able to
make your life miserable, just when you don't
need him to be shoving his ugly face into your
affairs. I would have tried to kick him too,
Max (though I would probably have missed,
however big the target), but I would have
regretted it afterward.

Do you think you might talk to Uncle Derek
or Pauline about how you feel? No one wants
you to be unhappy, especially not your mum,
and even James would be upset if he knew he
was making you unhappy. Perhaps Uncle
Derek or Pauline might be able to talk to your
mother for you.

Love, D.J.

Dear D.J.,

Mum keeps asking me what's wrong, and
I don't know what to say because *everything's*
wrong. I've made her all worried now because
she knows I'm hiding something. She asked if
I wanted her to stay in tonight, but I said I was
fine and that I wanted her to go out.

The Rabbit's here now. I've shut myself in
my room and told her that she can't stop me.
I don't think she cares anyway, because her
program's on TV.

I'm trying to think about my play so that I can
forget everything else. The gruesome ogre is so
angry at being shut in the cupboard without her
television that she has crashed her way out.
Fungus Face has managed to fool everyone that

he's not really dangerous and only wants to be loved. Everyone wants to be friends with him then, even Buster's friends. When they are left alone, Buster tries to persuade his mother to go with him, but his mother doesn't believe she's in danger because the wicked witch has cast a spell over her.

BUSTER: Fungus Face is up to no good, Mother. *(whispering)* Believe me, we must get rid of him for good.

BUSTER'S MUM: You're wrong, Buster. He wouldn't
hurt a fly.

BUSTER: He's fooling you, Mother. Come
with me now, before he can
do us any more harm. And
while that gruesome ogre is
watching TV.

BUSTER'S MUM: No, Buster, I am staying here.
Fungus Face is my friend.

BUSTER: Then I will go and fight the dragon
alone and hope that the Fat Knight
will wake up and protect you.

(He runs off.)

Love, Max

Dear D.J.,

It's even worse now. Baldychops is directing this
year's Christmas show at the theatre. They've
just started rehearsals and Mum's going to help
do the scenery and costumes. That means she'll
be out with him even more and I'll have to put
up with RABBIT RABBIT RABBIT even more.

Jenny keeps trying to talk to me at school
about Baldychops. She's says he's a bit dishy
and Mum's very lucky to have someone so
dishy, especially since he's younger than her.
And she says her mum says he'll soon get fed
up with having to deal with someone else's kid
when he hasn't got any kids of his own. Or he
might want to have his own kid with my mum
and then I won't be wanted as much. When
she said that, I couldn't help it, D.J., I got hold

of her ponytail and pulled it as hard as I could. Eggy came in when Ben was trying to stop me and he sent me to see the principal. Now the principal is going to write to Mum.

I'm in such big trouble, D.J. Nobody will want to speak to me now, especially Emily.

I hate everything and I feel like running away.

Love, Max

October 26

Dear Max,

If you run away, where will you run away to?
You'll be cold and scared and hungry, and
you'll have nowhere to sleep and nobody to
talk to. You'll miss your bed and your friends
and your teddy and your mum. Remember
what Buster says in your play: "Running away
is what cowards do."

Talk to your mother, Max. She'll be very
upset to know that you've been trying to
cope with your anxieties all on your own.

Love, D.J.

P.S. I ran away when I was about your age.
I got as far as the bottom of the road when
a tree made a great creaking noise and sent
me scuttling back home again.

Dear Max,
I'm worried because I
haven't heard from you.
Write soon and let
me Know how you are.
     Love, D.J.

Dear D.J.,

I ran away, D.J. Mrs. Rabbits was babysitting and
I packed a bag and sneaked out through the back
door. I forgot my coat and it was raining and it
was dark. I walked and walked and
walked and I kept
thinking that I wanted
Mum, but she wasn't at
home anyway. A big black dog
barked at me and made me jump and
a truck drove past and splashed me and I wanted
Mum even more, and
Dad, too. I wished
Dad was still alive
because then there
wouldn't have been
a Baldychops. I got so wet and cold, D.J., that
I wanted to go home again, but I'd lost my way.

Then a car came up. It was Baldychops's silly old sports car. Baldychops jumped out and asked me what I was doing, and I shouted at him, "Go away, just go away, it's all your fault." So he said, "I will go away, but not until I've taken you home. Your mother is worried sick about you." I wanted her so much that I got in the car. I didn't speak to him, but when we got to the house, Baldychops said, "I'd like to be your friend, Max," before he drove away.

I just cried and cried when I saw Mum. She gave me a big cuddle until I stopped, then she asked me what was wrong, and I told her what they were saying about Baldychops and having babies and not wanting me and being dropped from the soccer team, and Mum cried a bit too then, so I gave her a big cuddle. She said I was a silly

goose because I would always be the most important person in her life. Then she said that James was a very nice man and she enjoyed his company, but that it was still early days and that Jenny and her mum were just making mischief. Then I told her about Mrs. Rabbits and that I didn't like her—I had to explain who Mrs. Rabbits was because I forgot that was my name for her!—and Mum said that was lucky because Mrs. Rabbits had a Christmas job and was too tired to sit as well as working.

I feel better because Mum knows now, D.J., but I still wish it was just the two of us.

Love, Max

Dear D.J.,

Mum's been in to see the principal and she
spoke to Eggy and I think they gave Jenny a
big talking-to. Emily says she doesn't blame
me for what I did because Jenny was being
horrible.

I'm going to try really hard to be friends with
Baldychops for Mum's sake. I'm going to ask
him to help me with my play—I hope you
don't mind—and with my drawing. I'll have
to hurry up and finish my play now because
Eggy—he's all right, really—wants us to do it in
front of the little ones at the end of term.

Love, Max

November 10

Dear Max,

You sounded so much happier in your last
letter. I'm delighted that Mrs. Rabbits has
disappeared back down her burrow. Now that
you're feeling happier, I'm sure you'll race
ahead with your play—especially with
James's help.

I've raced ahead with *Where There's a Will*.
One more chapter to go and it's finished.
I have no idea what I'll be writing about next.
I'm hoping that inspiration will hit me while
I'm leopard-spotting in South Africa. In fact, it
would make a change for me to write about
animals rather than people.

Love, D.J.

Dear D.J.,

Why don't you write about meerkats?
Meerkats are amazing. Some of them go
on sentry duty, and some of them act as
babysitters! I'd rather have a meerkat
babysitting than a rabbit! Uncle Derek and
Pauline have babysat the last two times and
Scallywag came with them. He chewed the
nose of the lion mask Mum had made for
Baldychops's play and Mum
wasn't very happy, but
I thought it was funny.

Baldychops is coming
for lunch tomorrow.
I'm going to try to
be friendly.

Love, Max

Dear D.J.,

You'll never guess what. Baldychops wants me
to be in his Christmas show! Me! It's called
The Wizard of Oz and he wants me to be
a Munchkin, whatever that is. There's one
Munchkin who has some words to say and
he says I'll be perfect for it. I couldn't believe
he wanted me to be in it, and then I thought
I'd be far too scared. But Baldychops said he
knows from Mum that I'm a big brave boy so
he's sure I can do it.

I said yes, D.J., and I've got to go to rehearsals
on a Saturday afternoon, and Mum's going to
help me learn my lines and make my costume.
Now I've got two plays to work on—my own
and Baldychops's.

Love, Max

P.S. Baldychops did the drawing on the back of this letter. (I didn't want him to know that I call him Baldychops, so I turned it over!) It's what I will look like as a Munchkin.

November 22

Dear Munchkin,

That's wonderful news, Max. I love *The Wizard of Oz*, it's such a magical play. You'll have great fun rehearsing for it. You'll be so busy learning your lines and finishing your own play that you won't have time to write to me!

I've finished *Where There's a Will* and I've sent it off to my publisher. Fingers crossed! Now I've got to spend the next week touring round bookshops to sign more copies of *My Teacher's a Nutcase* before the film comes out. Sadly, I'm not visiting a bookshop near you, but at least you've got a signed copy of the book already.

I hope everything's all right at school now.

Love, D.J.

P.S. Enclosed with this letter are six tickets for you and your family and friends to see *My Teacher's a Nutcase* at the big movie theater in your town.

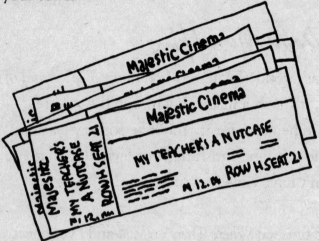

Dear D.J.,

Well done, D.J. You've finished it at last! I can't wait to read it.

Thank you **sooooooooo** much for the tickets. I can't wait! I'm going to take Mum and Uncle Derek and Pauline and Ben, and I'm going to ask Emily but I haven't yet. Mum's going to write to you as well.

I've got a new babysitter. She's from Mum's work and her name's Marsha and she says it's all right if I call her Marshmallow. She's really cool, D.J. This is a picture of her.

She likes playing computer games, so I've got someone to play with now. (Mum and Baldychops are hopeless at them.) And she's been listening to me say my Munchkin lines, and she says she's going to help me make masks for my play (I'm not going to have costumes, except for a tail on the dragon) because Mum and Baldychops are a bit too busy at the moment.

I've nearly finished my play. Fungus Face and the gruesome ogre and the wicked witch are going to be frightened away by Buster riding on the dragon's back.
Buster makes the dragon some toast and Buster's mum comes back from her spell. I want Baldychops to make the dragon mask, and he says he will.

I'm going to my first rehearsal on Saturday and I'm really nervous. I hope Baldychops doesn't decide that I'm useless.

Love, Max

November 29

Dear Max,

I'm going to the premiere of My *Teacher's*
a Nutcase in London tonight and I'm petrified.
All the stars will be there, and we have to walk
into the theater along a red carpet laid out on
the pavement with all the television and
newspaper cameras pointed at us. I've told
Christopher he will have to hold on to me
tightly because I shall probably faint from
fright. I've had to buy a new fancy dress, but
I shall probably still look very frumpy alongside
Jennifer Aniseed. Thank goodness we're going
away very soon. At least there won't be any
press on safari.

Wish me luck that my high heels don't catch in the carpet.

Love, D.J.

P.S. The new babysitter sounds great!

P.P.S. Good luck with the rehearsal, Max.

Dear D.J.,

I saw you on TV! I was watching it with
Mum and Baldychops and suddenly there
you were! I crossed my fingers that you
wouldn't trip up.

Yesterday I asked Emily if she would like to
come to *My Teacher's a Nutcase* with me, and I
said that Ben's coming as well. She said she'd
love to, and then I wanted to ask if she would

be my girlfriend, but that was more scary than standing up in front of everybody. The words just wouldn't come out.

Love, Max

P.S. Jenny still tries to make mischief at school, but I just ignore her.

Dear D.J.,

We're going to do my play on the last day of
term. I've finished writing it and Baldychops
has helped me make a few bits better, and
Marshmallow and I have nearly finished all the
masks. The dragon mask Baldychops has made
is fantastico. I can't wait to wear it. We're
rehearsing at school next week with the rest
of my friends, and Ben says I mustn't worry
what Jenny and Huge Bigbottom think, so
I won't.

Love, Max

P.S. The premiere of *The Wizard of
Oz* is just after Christmas.
I can't wait to walk on
the red carpet! Hee hee!

December 8

Dear Max,

We're away to South Africa in six days' time. Congratulations on finishing *Buster and the Dragon*. I hope you'll send me a signed copy!

I hope you all enjoy *My Teacher's a Nutcase*. I had a wonderful time at the premiere, even though I was dreading it. Perhaps I can cope with being a little bit of a superstar, as long as I can run away afterward.

It'll be your turn to be a little bit of a superstar when you perform *Buster and the Dragon*. And then you'll be a superstar for a second time in *The Wizard of Oz*. You deserve it, Max. Enjoy every minute of it.

Love, D.J.

Dear D.J.,

Before you go, do you think you might be able
to send me one more ticket for *My Teacher's
a Nutcase*? I know I'm being cheeky, but I think
James might like to come.

Love, Max

At Heathrow

Bravo, Max!

One more ticket enclosed.
Good Luck to the Munchkin
and the Dragon
Have a Wonderful Christmas
Love, D.J.

Majestic
MY TEACHER'S
A NUTCASE
ROW H SEAT 27